MOLLY ROGERS

PIRATE GIRL

For Lucan Rocco Wood, my favourite beach companion – C.F.

For Marta and Natalia. And pirate girls everywhere – K.M.

Published in 2021 in Great Britain by
Barrington Stoke Ltd
18 Walker Street, Edinburgh, EH3 7LP

www.barringtonstoke.co.uk

This edition based on *Molly Rogers, Pirate Girl*
(Barrington Stoke, 2017)

This story was originally published in a different form
in a German edition: *Käpten Knitterbart und seine Bande*

A CIP catalogue record for this book is available from the British Library upon request

ISBN: 978-1-80090-079-0

Printed by Hussar Books, Poland

Molly Rogers

Pirate Girl

Cornelia Funke

Illustrated by
Kasia Matyjaszek

Captain Firebeard and his crew were the terror of the seas.

When people spotted his ship, the *Horrible Haddock*, their knees shook like jelly.

But one day Captain Firebeard robbed a ship he should have left alone.

On board was a girl named Molly, who was on her way to see her grandma.

Molly hid, but one of the pirates found her. "What shall we do with her?" he asked.

"Take her with us!" Captain Firebeard bellowed. "Her parents can pay to get her back!"

"You'll be sorry for this!" Molly cried.

"Tell me your parents' names!" growled Captain Firebeard.

"No!" Molly growled back. "If I told you my mother's name, you'd be so scared you'd cry like a baby!"

All the pirates howled with laughter.

So they put Molly to work. She peeled the potatoes. She scrubbed the decks. She mended the sails.

Soon every bone in her body hurt.

But when Captain Firebeard asked for her parents' names again, Molly just smiled.

Every night, the pirates had a party.

They drank rum and sang rude songs.

One night the pirates partied until dawn, then fell asleep on the deck.

Molly tiptoed to the side of the ship and threw a bottle into the sea.

Splash!

"Hey! What was that?" Captain Firebeard yelled.

"It's a message in a bottle!" the other pirates cried.

“Bring it to me!” Captain Firebeard shouted.

The pirates jumped into the sea. They looked for the bottle, but it had bobbed away.

"What did you write?" Captain Firebeard growled.

But Molly just kicked his wooden leg.

"Time to feed her to the sharks!" Captain Firebeard roared.

But the look-out shouted, “Stop! Ship ahoy!”

A ship was speeding towards them. A pirate ship with red sails.

“It’s Barbarous Bertha!” the crew wailed.

“That’s my mum!” Molly grinned.

Captain Firebeard and his pirate crew groaned with terror. Now their knees shook like jelly.

Barbarous Bertha and her crew jumped on board the *Horrible Haddock* with a roar.

"We got your message, my pirate girl!" Barbarous Bertha cried. "Now, how can we punish these pirates?"

"Well!" said Molly. "That's easy."

After that, Captain Firebeard and his pirate crew had no time to rob ships.

They scrubbed the deck.

They peeled potatoes.

Captain Firebeard polished Barbarous Bertha's boots fourteen times a week.

And at last Molly visited her grandma!

HAVE YOU READ THEM ALL?

Cornelia Funke
Gawain Greytail
and the Terrible Tab

MOLLY ROGERS
PIRATE GIRL
Cornelia Funke
Illustrated by Kasia Matyjaszek

ALEXANDER McCALL SMITH
BOING BOING
ILLUSTRATED BY
ZOE PERSICO

Michael Rosen
Illustrated by Richard Watson
Mad IN THE Back

MICHAEL ROSEN
Wolfman
Illustrated by Chris Mould

ELEANOR UPDALE
Illustrated by Sarah Horne
Itch Scritch Scratch

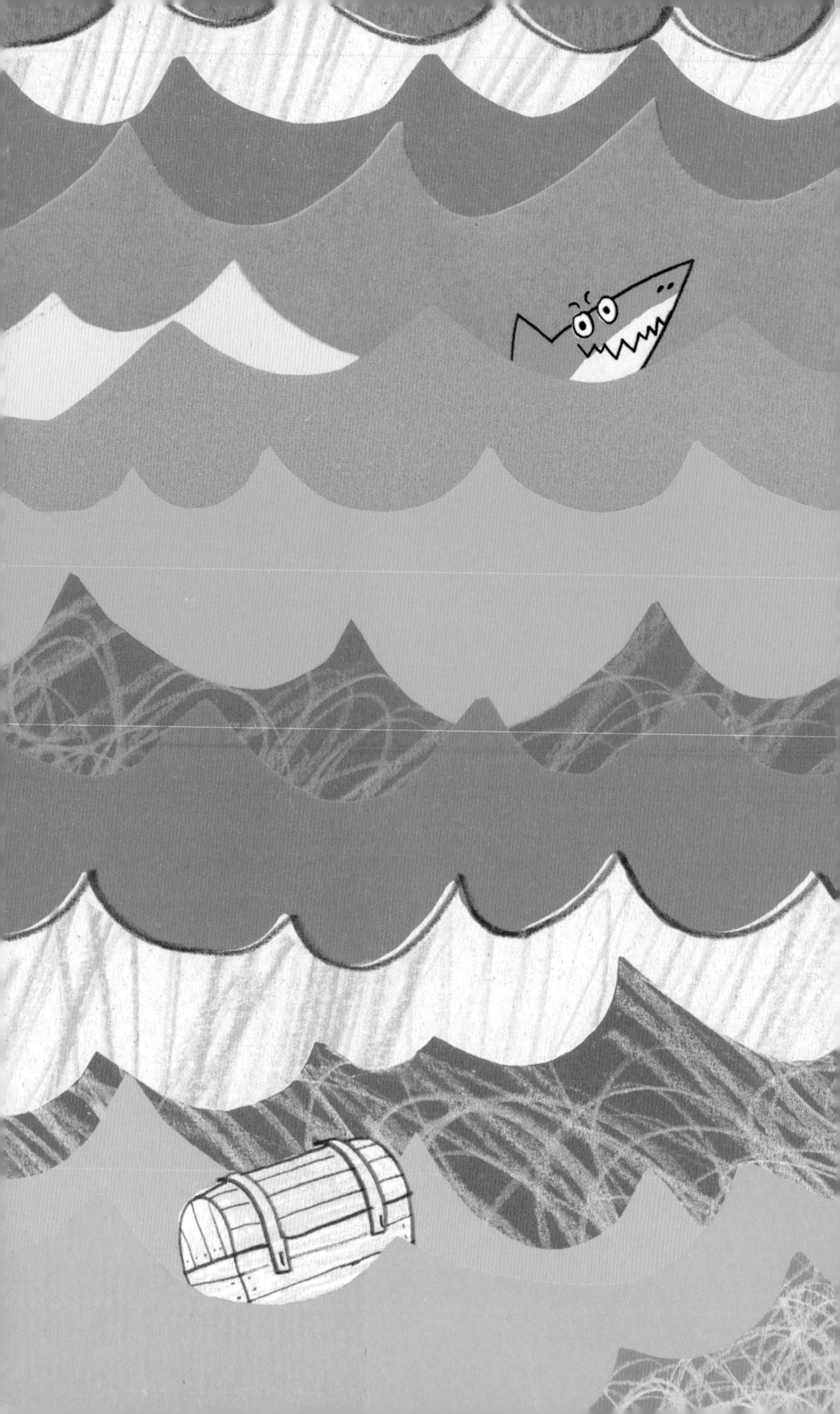